BABY-O

Words by **Nancy White Carlstrom**

Pictures by **Suçie Stevenson**

Little, Brown and Company

Boston   Toronto   London

First Edition

Library of Congress Cataloging-in-Publication Data

Carlstrom, Nancy White.
    Baby-O / words by Nancy White Carlstrom ; pictures by Suçie
Stevenson. — 1st ed.
        p.   cm.
    Summary: Three generations of a West Indian family gather together
on a jitney that takes them and their wares to the local market.
    ISBN 0-316-12851-1
    [1. Markets — Fiction.   2. Rural families — Fiction.   3. Caribbean
Area — Fiction.   4. Stories in rhyme.]   I. Stevenson, Suçie, ill.
II. Title.
PZ8.3.C1948Bab   1992
[E] — dc20   90-45975

10 9 8 7 6 5 4 3 2 1

WOR

Published simultaneously in Canada
by Little, Brown & Company (Canada) Limited

Printed in the United States of America

For the Trautmans
Chris and Jeff, Sarah and Rachel

In celebration of friendship and island times.
— N.W.C.

For Jim Johnston
— S.S.

Chickens running in the garden patch,
Running in the morning sun.
Try and catch.
Chuka Chuka
Chuka Chuka

Sing a song of Baby-O,
Sing it soft, now, sing it slow.
Chuka Chuka

Listen to the way our baby goes,
Baby Baby Baby-O.

New cloth soaking in the big tin tub,
Soaking in the morning sun.
Wash and rub.
Wusha Wusha
Wusha Wusha

Sing a song of Mama-O,
Sing it soft, now, sing it slow.
Wusha Wusha

Listen to the way our mama goes,
Mama Mama Mama-O.

Small truck rolling down the brown dirt road,
Rolling in the morning sun.
Carry a load.
Tomatoma
Tomatoma

Sing a song of Brother-O,
Sing it soft, now, sing it slow.
T o m a t o m a

Listen to the way our brother goes,
Brother Brother Brother-O.

Long hoe digging up the stubborn weeds,
Digging in the morning sun.
Help those seeds.
Kongada
Kongada

Sing a song of Pappy-O,
Sing it soft, now, sing it slow.
K o n g a d a

Listen to the way our pappy goes,
Pappy Pappy Pappy-O.

Mangoes falling from the tree way high,
Falling in the morning sun.
Laughing at the sky.
Pika Pika
Pika Pika

Sing a song of Sister-O,
Sing it soft, now, sing it slow.
P i k a P i k a

Sing a song of Granny-O,
Sing it soft, now, sing it slow.
P l e s h   P l e s h

Listen to the way our granny goes,
Granny Granny Granny-O.

Great nets fishing off the sandy shore,
Fishing in the morning sun.
Get plenty more.
Dippa Dippa
Dippa Dippa

Sing a song of Papa-O,
Sing it soft, now, sing it slow.
D i p p a   D i p p a

Listen to the way our papa goes,
Papa Papa Papa-O.

Chuka Chuka, Wusha Wusha
Tomatoma, Kongada
Pika Pika, Plesh Plesh
Dippa Dippa

Sing a song of Family-O,

Sing it soft, now, sing it slow.

Chuka Chuka Wusha Wusha
Tomatoma Kongada
Pika Pika Plesh Plesh
Dippa Dippa

Listen to the way our family goes,
Family Family Family-O.

Jitney chugging to the market town,
Over the mountainside.
Up and down.
Putta Putta Clank Clank
Putta Putta Clank Clank

Sing a song of Baby-O,
Sing it loud, now, watch it grow.

Chuka Chuka, Wusha Wusha, Tomatoma, Kongada

Pika Pika, Plesh Plesh, Dippa Dippa

Putta Putta Clank Clank
Putta Putta Clank Clank

Listen to the way the Baby goes,
Baby Baby Baby-O.